Sofia the First

Riches to Rags

Adapted by Susan Amerikaner

Based on the episode "The Baker King," by Laurie Israel and Rachel Ruderman

Illustrated by Character Building Studio and the Disney Storybook Art Team

ABDOBOOKS.COM

Reinforced library bound edition published in 2019 by Spotlight, a division of ABDO, PO Box 398166, Minneapolis, Minnesota 55439. Spotlight produces high-quality reinforced library bound editions for schools and libraries. Published by agreement with Disney Press, an imprint of Disney Book Group.

Printed in the United States of America, North Mankato, Minnesota.
092018   012019

DISNEY PRESS
New York • Los Angeles

THIS BOOK CONTAINS RECYCLED MATERIALS

Library of Congress Control Number: 2017961288

Publisher's Cataloging-in-Publication Data

Names: Amerikaner, Susan, author. | Isreal, Laurie, author. | Ruderman, Rachel, author. | Character Building Studio, Disney Storybook Art Team, illustrators.
Title: Sofia the First: Riches to rags / by Susan Amerikaner, Laurie Israel and Rachel Ruderman; illustrated by Character Building Studio and Disney Storybook Art Team.
Description: Minneapolis, MN : Spotlight, 2019 | Series: World of reading level 1
Summary: When King Roland wishes in a magic mirror that he could trade places with a baker, the royal family find themselves running the village bakery. He learns that being a baker is no piece of cake.
Identifiers: ISBN 9781532141966 (lib. bdg.)
Subjects: LCSH: Sofia the First (Television program)--Juvenile fiction. | Kings, queens, rulers, etc.--Juvenile fiction. | Wishes--Juvenile fiction. | Bakers and bakeries--Juvenile fiction. | Readers (Primary)--Juvenile fiction.
Classification: DDC [E]--dc23

Spotlight
A Division of ABDO
abdobooks.com

Sofia is happy.
It is almost time for the Villagers'
Ball.

Violet will go to the ball.
She helps Sofia get dressed.

The king has lots to do before
the ball.
He must open the new school.

He must fix the playground.
The garden needs work, too.
The king is very busy.

Sofia wants to help.
She helps the king choose
the new court jester.

The king has more to do.
He orders the cake for the ball.
"A baker does not work this hard,"
he says.

"I wish I were a baker."

The next day Sofia wakes up.
She is not in the castle.

Her family is in the village!

A man comes to buy bread.
"But I'm the king," says the king.
"Ha-ha!" says the man. "You are
the village baker!"

"Dad made a wish in front of the magic mirror," says Sofia.
"We must break the spell," says Amber.

But the king still wants to be a baker.
"I will not be so busy," he says.
"All I have to do is bake."

Sofia and the queen teach
everyone how to bake.

The king makes a big mess!
He tries again.

A mom stops to buy bread.

She pays too much!

Sofia finds the mom.
She returns some money.

The mom says everyone loves the
king for the new playground.
He needs to know this!
Sofia has a plan.

Sofia and the king go out.
They visit the playground.
They see the garden he grew.
What a happy village!

But the teacher at school is
not happy.
"The king did not come to open
the school," she says.

The king feels bad.
He must fix this.
"Time to break the spell," he says.
"How?" says Amber.

The king must go to the castle.
He must get to the magic mirror.
He must wish to be king again.

But first there is work to do.
The baker must make the cake for
the ball.
"We will bring it to you soon,"
says Sofia.

"This will be hard work," says the queen.

"A hard job is worth doing!" says the king.

The cake is ready!
They bring it to the castle.

Sofia and the king go to the
magic mirror.
The king wishes to be king again.
The spell is broken!

The people cheer.
The king is happy.
It is time for cake!

"This cake tastes bad," says the king.
"We must talk to the baker!"
Sofia and the king smile.